ESCAPE FROM PLANET

ALCATRAZ

THE CRUSHING CRYSTALS

BY MICHAEL DAHL

ILLUSTRATED BY SHEN FEI

raintree

a Capstone company — publishers for children

Raintree is an imprint of Capstone Global Library Limited, a company incorporated in England and Wales having its registered office at 264 Banbury Road, Oxford, OX2 7DY – Registered company number: 6695582

www.raintree.co.uk
myorders@raintree.co.uk

Text © Capstone Global Library Limited 2020
The moral rights of the proprietor have been asserted.

Edited by Aaron J Sautter
Designed by Kay Fraser
Original illustrations © Capstone Global Library Limited 2020
Production by Katy LaVigne
Originated by Capstone Global Library Ltd
Printed and bound in India

ISBN: 978 1 4747 8494 8 (paperback)

British Library Cataloguing in Publication Data
A full catalogue record for this book is available from the British Library.

Acknowledgements
Design elements: Shutterstock: Agustina Camilion, A-Star, Dima Zel, Draw_Wing_Zen, Hybrid_Graphics, Metallic Citizen

CONTENTS

ERRO

PLATEAU OF LENG

PHANTOM FOREST

POISON SEA

VULCAN MOUNTAINS

LAKE OF GOLD

METAL MOON

DIAMOND MINES

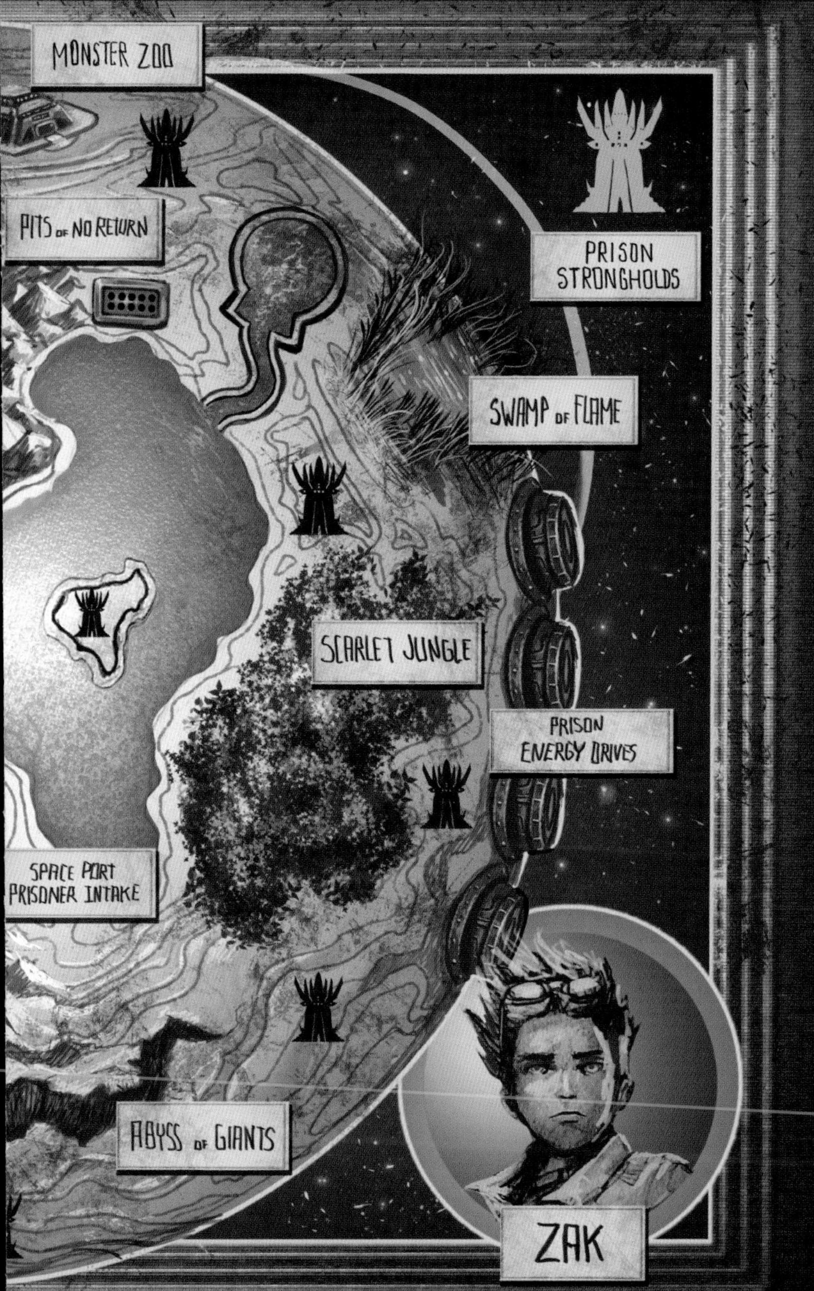

MONSTER ZOO

PITS OF NO RETURN

PRISON STRONGHOLDS

SWAMP OF FLAME

SCARLET JUNGLE

PRISON ENERGY DRIVES

SPACE PORT PRISONER INTAKE

ABYSS OF GIANTS

ZAK

THE PRISONERS

ZAK NINE

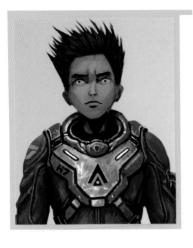

Zak is a teenage boy from Earth Base Zeta. He dreams of piloting a star fighter one day. Zak is very brave and is a quick thinker. But his enthusiasm often leads him into trouble.

ERRO

Erro is a teenage furling from the planet Quom. He has the fur, long tail, sharp eyes and claws of his species. Erro is often impatient with Zak's reckless ways. But he shares his friend's love of adventure.

THE PRISON PLANET

Alcatraz . . . there is no escape from this terrifying prison planet. It's filled with dungeons, traps, endless deserts and other dangers. Zak Nine and his alien friend, Erro, are trapped here. They had sneaked onto a ship hoping to see an awesome space battle. But the ship landed on Alcatraz instead. Now they have to work together if they ever hope to escape!

ZAK'S STORY . . . ON THE RUN >>>

We've been running for days through this giant desert. A few nights ago Erro and I found an electronic map device in an empty old spaceship. Erro thinks it will lead us to a safe hiding place. But I just hope we can avoid getting caught by Alcatraz's robot guards. . . .

>>>>

CHAPTER ONE:
THE FREEZING DARK

Alcatraz's robot guards have been trailing us for days.

The desert sky is as dark as a whomp bat. The wind bites through my thin clothes. The blowing sand feels like ice.

Erro is lucky. He's got fur. He can stay warm here on the windy plain.

But I'm freezing! All the walking
we've done hasn't warmed me up at all.

At least the map device in my hand is warm. We found it in a crashed prison ship two days ago.

"Is the device still working?" Erro asks.

"It's still glowing green," I say. I think that has to be a good sign.

Maybe the map can show us how to get across this strange, flat land.

The map calls this area the Plateau of Leng. Maybe we can cross it before the robots find us. They're only just over a kilometre away.

I don't want to see their wicked metal claws again.

A pale light is growing in the distance. The sun will be up soon. Then the guards will easily see us in this empty place.

"We need to hurry," I tell Erro.

Erro leaps across the sandy land.
He can easily jump a couple of metres
at a time. The guy acts like it's nothing.

I'm rushing to catch up. But it's not
easy to read the map and run at the
same time.

CHAPTER TWO:
THE PLATEAU OF LENG

Suddenly I see something on the map about the local animal life.

"Wait, Erro!" I yell out. "The map says there are scorpion rats!"

Erro stops and looks back at me. He looks scared. "Did you say . . . rats?" he asks.

At that moment, a ray of sunlight pierces the sky. We hear a loud rumble. The ground begins shaking beneath our feet.

Suddenly we hear a crash. Erro and I spin around to look behind us.

We stare in awe as a gleaming mountain shoots up from the ground. It looks like it's made of ice or glass. The jagged shapes are a rainbow of colour.

"Crystal," says Erro. "A mountain of crystal!"

KRRRRRAAAAAACCKK!

Another mountain of crystal rises up next to the first one. Sand from the desert spills down its sides.

The gleaming shapes form a huge wall between us and the robot guards.

"Yes!" I shout. "Those robots won't get through that crystal wall."

The rising crystal walls grind and crush against each other. Bright chunks break off and fall to the ground.

"Look out!" cries Erro.

"What–?" I start to say. But then he shoves me to the side.

THUD!

A huge chunk of sparkling crystal lands right in front of me.

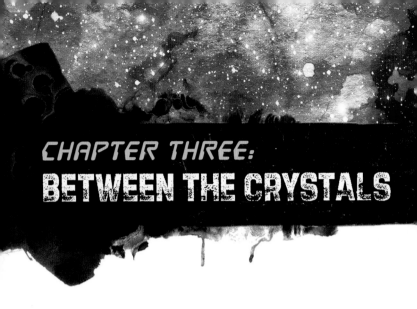

CHAPTER THREE:
BETWEEN THE CRYSTALS

The morning sun is now higher in the sky. New cliffs of crystal continue rising up around us.

"Oh no! We're being surrounded!" I shout.

"Look," Erro says, pointing. "I think it is the sun. The sunlight is making the crystals grow."

He's right. The crystals keep growing
wherever rays of sunshine touch them.
It looks like bubbling glass.

Then I see a narrow gap between two
mountains ahead of us.

The gap between the mountains is in shadow. It should stay open if the sunlight doesn't reach it – I hope.

Erro and I run as fast as we can.

"The gap is getting smaller!"
Erro shouts. "We will not make it!"

"Oh, yes we will, fur boy!" I shout
back. "Keep running!"

Sunlight reflects off the crystal walls behind us. As the walls grow higher, the light races across the sand beside us.

Everywhere the sun touches, smaller crystals begin to bubble up.

Erro looks at me with his wide yellow eyes. We both know what will happen if the beams of sunlight reach the gap.

We race faster and faster.

CHAPTER FOUR:
A TIGHT SQUEEZE

Erro and I reach the gap and squeeze through the opening.

The walls on either side press inwards on us. The sharp, glassy walls rip my clothes as we move forward.

Just as we reach the end of the passage, bright-red sunlight sparkles behind us!

KRAACKKKKKKK!

New slabs of sharp red crystal smash against each other. They fill up the gap, and the passage is gone!

"See? We made it," I say to Erro, breathing heavily.

But my alien friend's tail is twitching again. Something is wrong.

I follow his eyes and see something golden. It's rising up out of a hole in the sand.

Is that another crystal wall? I think.

No – it's a big yellow scorpion with the face of a rat!

CHAPTER FIVE:
CRACK!

We stand there, staring at the scorpion.

The wicked creature stares back, clicking its huge claws. Its deadly tail slowly rises over its body.

The sun is higher in the sky now. More crystal cliffs are rising all around us. Chunks of broken crystal fall to the ground like meteors.

CRRUUNNCH!

KRASSSSSSSHHH!

In a moment, we'll be trapped inside with the monster.

Erro suddenly looks up and then back at the scorpion. Then he starts waving his arms at the creature.

"Over here!" he shouts.

"Are you crazy?" I yell.

The scorpion skitters towards us on its clicking legs. Its rat-like mouth opens, and we see rows of sharp yellow teeth.

Erro and I back up against the crystal wall. With the gap closed, there is no escape.

"When we pulled the cages closer, the spheres started pushing each other," I explain. "They're repelling each other, like magnets. That's what's making them move."

"Look! We are starting to move across the sea!" says Erro.

Behind us, many other cages are swinging now. The other prisoners are copying our escape attempt.

We stare down at the bubbling yellow waves passing beneath us.

"There's got to be a shore somewhere," I say.

Clouds of yellow mist soon surround our cages.

"Careful of the poison," I say.

We wrap our cloaks around our mouths and noses.

"See anything?" I ask Erro. His Quom eyes are a lot sharper than mine.

Erro nods. "I think there is a large–"

CLANG!

We hit a rocky cliff.

Both of us drop out of our cages and slide down a long, sandy slope.

We end up on a beach. The yellow waves are a couple of metres away. Then we spot a pair of red eyes staring at us hungrily.

"Hurry! Off the beach!" I shout. We both run from the yellow acid as fast as we can.

"I am starving," says Erro.

"Me too. Let's find something to eat,"
I say. "And somewhere safe to hide from
the Alcatraz guards. . ."

GLOSSARY

anti-gravity fictional force that works against the force of gravity to push things away

canyon deep, narrow valley with steep sides, often with a stream or river running through it

dungeon prison, usually underground

hover ship fictional vehicle that travels through the air using anti-gravity

magnet piece of metal that has two ends called poles; the same poles push two magnets apart, while different poles pull them together

repel push something away

species group of living things that share similar features

sphere round, solid shape such as a football or globe

TALK ABOUT IT

1. When Erro climbs outside his cage, he is nearly eaten by a huge sea monster. Do you think any creature could actually live in a sea of poison acid? Explain your answer.

2. Zak tells Erro to touch the glowing sphere, but Erro is scared to do it at first. If a friend asked you to do something that seemed dangerous, would you do it?

3. Zak and Erro have to work together to escape the poison sea. Can you think of any other ways the boys could escape their cages and reach dry land without the guards finding them?

WRITE ABOUT IT

1. At the start of the story, Zak and Erro have been captured by the Alcatraz guards. How do you think the boys were caught? Use your imagination to write your own version of how the boys were captured.

2. Imagine you are a prisoner in one of the other cages hanging over the poison sea. How did you end up on the prison planet? In your own words, tell the story of how you became a prisoner on Alcatraz and how you would escape from your cage.

ABOUT THE AUTHOR

Michael Dahl is the author of more than 300 books for young readers, including the Library of Doom series. He is a huge fan of Star Trek, Star Wars and Doctor Who. He has a fear of closed-in spaces, but has visited several prisons, dungeons and strongholds, both ancient and modern. He made a daring escape from each one. Luckily, the guards still haven't found him.

ABOUT THE ILLUSTRATOR

Shen Fei loved comic books as a child. By the age of five he began making his own comic books and drawing scenes from his favourite films. After graduating from art school he worked in the entertainment industry, creating art for films, games and books. Shen currently lives in Malaysia and works as a freelance illustrator for publishers all over the world. He also teaches at a local art school as a guest lecturer.